Pawns
of
Power

Rachael Reed
©2024

Chapter 1: The Game Begins

Norfolk, Virginia, wasn't just a city; it was a battleground, a place where survival meant more than just getting by. It meant thriving in a world where the stakes were as high as the skyscrapers that loomed over the gritty streets. In the midst of it all were Omar and Mona, two souls caught up in the whirlwind of the drug game, where dreams were made and shattered in the blink of an eye.

Omar, known on the streets as O, was the kind of man who commanded respect. His rise from a small-time hustler to a millionaire drug dealer was the stuff of legends. Flipping kilos with ease, he built an empire that stretched across the city, his name whispered in awe and fear. At thirty-two, Omar had it all—money, power, and a reputation that made him untouchable. His days were filled with deals and dollars, his nights with luxury and indulgence. He drove the latest Benz, his wrist glinted with a Rolex, and his pockets were always full.

But behind every kingpin was a queen, and for Omar, that queen was Mona. At twenty-eight, Mona was as fierce as she was beautiful. Her caramel skin glowed, and her curves were the envy of every woman who laid eyes on her. But it wasn't just her looks that kept Omar captivated—it was her loyalty. Mona had stood by Omar through thick and thin, through the good times and the bad. She was his ride or die, the one who made sure the house was in order while he handled business on the streets.

Mona's life revolved around Omar. She loved the man, but she also loved the lifestyle—the house, the car, the money. She had grown accustomed to the finer things, and she wasn't about to let them slip through her fingers. Her days were spent maintaining their lavish home, shopping for the latest fashions, and making sure she looked the part of a drug dealer's queen. Her nights were spent waiting for Omar to come home, the anxiety of the streets always lurking in the back of her mind.

The allure of the drug game was seductive. The money came fast and easy, the respect was instantaneous, and the power was intoxicating. But it was a double-edged sword, and Mona knew it. For every high, there was a low. For every gain, there was a loss. She had seen friends gunned down, associates locked up for life, and families torn apart. But she couldn't walk away. The game had its claws in her, just as it did in Omar.

Omar's empire was built on trust and fear. He surrounded himself with a tight-knit crew who knew the rules: loyalty above all else. Big D was his right-hand man, a hulking presence with a fierce loyalty to Omar. Together, they navigated the treacherous waters of the drug trade, dealing with rival dealers, police crackdowns, and the constant threat of betrayal.

But it wasn't just the police Omar had to worry about. The streets were buzzing with the emergence of the Junior Mafia, a ruthless gang known for their extortion tactics. They had set their sights on Omar's empire, demanding a cut of his profits. Omar knew he couldn't back down—any sign of weakness and his empire would crumble. But he also knew the Junior Mafia was not to be trifled with. Their leader, Rico, was as cold-blooded as they came, and he played for keeps.

Mona felt the pressure too. She knew Omar was under constant threat, and it scared her. The more powerful he became, the more dangerous their lives got. She tried to push the fear aside, focusing on the good things—the money, the luxury, the status. But at night, when the city was quiet and Omar was out handling business, the fear crept back in. She worried about losing everything—their house, their car, their money, and most of all, Omar.

The seductive allure of the drug game was a constant presence in their lives. It promised wealth and power but demanded a steep price. Omar thrived on it, his ambition and drive pushing him to the top. But Mona saw the darker side—the violence, the danger, the constant threat of losing it all. She knew the game had no mercy, and it scared her.

Yet, she couldn't walk away. The game was in their blood, a part of who they were. Omar's empire was built on the backs of those who had fallen before him, and Mona's life was intertwined with his. They were caught in the vicious cycle of the drug game, where every victory was shadowed by the threat of defeat.

As the sun set over Norfolk, casting long shadows over the city, Omar and Mona stood on the precipice of a new chapter. The game was about to get more dangerous, the stakes higher than ever. But for now, they had each other, and that was enough. Together, they would face whatever came their way, their love and loyalty the only constants in a world of chaos.

This was their life. These were their streets. And this was just the beginning.

Chapter 2: Life in the Fast Lane

The neon lights of Norfolk's skyline lit up the night, casting a vibrant glow over the city. For Omar and Mona, this was their playground, a world where luxury and danger intertwined. Life in the fast lane was exhilarating and perilous, filled with high-end parties, flashy cars, and the constant threat of violence.

Omar cruised through the streets in his sleek, black Benz, the engine purring like a predator. The leather seats were as smooth as his moves in the drug game. Mona sat beside him, her caramel skin glowing under the streetlights, her hair cascading in waves. She exuded confidence, but her eyes betrayed a flicker of anxiety. The streets were unpredictable, and even a moment of carelessness could turn their world upside down.

Tonight, they were heading to one of the city's most exclusive clubs, a hotspot for the elite of Norfolk's underworld. Omar parked the car, tossing the keys to the valet without a second glance. They walked into the club, the bass from the music vibrating through the floor. The air was thick with the scent of expensive perfume and the unmistakable tang of power.

"Yo, O!" Big D's booming voice cut through the noise. Omar's right-hand man was hard to miss, with his massive frame and fierce presence. He approached them, a grin splitting his face. "You ready to do this?"

Omar nodded, his eyes scanning the room. "Always, man. Let's make it a night to remember."

Mona trailed behind, catching sight of her best friend, Tasha, at the bar. Tasha was a force of nature, her laughter loud and infectious, her curves draped in a dress that screamed confidence. She waved Mona over, her eyes sparkling with excitement.

"Girl, you lookin' fine tonight!" Tasha exclaimed, pulling Mona into a hug. "How you been?"

Mona smiled, though her mind was preoccupied. "I'm good, Tasha. Just trying to keep up with O's lifestyle, you know?"

Tasha nodded, her expression turning serious. "Yeah, I feel you. This life ain't easy, but we gotta hold on to what we got."

The night unfolded in a haze of lights, music, and expensive champagne. Omar and Big D held court in the VIP section, discussing business with other major players in the drug game. Deals were made with a handshake and a knowing glance, the language of the streets spoken in hushed tones.

Mona and Tasha mingled with the crowd, their laughter masking the tension that simmered beneath the surface. Mona couldn't shake the feeling that something was about to go down. The constant threat of violence was a shadow that never left her side.

As the night wore on, the club grew louder, the crowd more animated. Omar kept a watchful eye on everything, his instincts honed by years of navigating this dangerous world. Big D leaned in, his voice a low rumble.

"Word is the Junior Mafia's been making moves. We gotta stay sharp, O."

Omar's jaw tightened. The Junior Mafia was a threat he couldn't afford to ignore. "We'll deal with them. But not tonight. Tonight, we enjoy ourselves."

Mona overheard their conversation, her anxiety spiking. She forced herself to smile, to keep up the façade of carefree luxury. But the reality of their lives was never far from her mind.

As the night drew to a close, Omar and Mona slipped out of the club, the cool night air a welcome relief. They drove home in silence, each lost in their own thoughts. The flashy cars and high-end parties were the glamorous side of their lives, but the danger was always lurking, a constant reminder of the cost of their choices.

Back at their house, a lavish mansion on the outskirts of the city, Mona finally let her guard down. She kicked off her heels and sank into the plush couch, her mind racing. Omar joined her, his expression unreadable.

"You okay, Mona?" he asked, his voice softening.

She nodded, though her heart was heavy. "Yeah, just thinking about everything. This life... it's not easy, O."

Omar sighed, running a hand through his hair. "I know. But it's the life we chose. And we gotta play it the best we can."

Mona reached out, taking his hand. "I just want us to be safe, to hold on to what we've got."

Omar squeezed her hand, his eyes locking onto hers. "We will. I promise."

The promise hung in the air, fragile and uncertain. In the world they lived in, safety was a luxury they couldn't always afford. But for now, they had each other, and that was enough.

The next day, the hustle continued. Omar and Big D were back to making moves, ensuring their empire stayed strong. Tasha visited Mona, their conversation turning to the dangers that seemed to grow with each passing day.

"Do you ever think about getting out?" Tasha asked, her tone serious.

Mona sighed. "All the time. But it's not that easy. O's in deep, and so am I. This life... it's got its claws in us."

Tasha nodded. "I know. But maybe one day, we'll find a way out."

Mona could only hope. For now, they were in the fast lane, living a life of luxury and danger, navigating the highs and lows with resilience and determination. The allure of the drug game was powerful, but so was their will to survive. And as long as they had that, they knew they could face whatever came their way.

Chapter 3: The Junior Mafia

The streets of Norfolk were buzzing with a new kind of fear. Whispers of the Junior Mafia had spread like wildfire, a ruthless gang known for their extortion and brutality. Omar had built his empire with blood and sweat, but now it was under siege from this rising threat.

Omar sat in his office, the room dimly lit, the weight of his empire pressing down on him. He leaned back in his chair, his fingers steepled as he considered his next move. Big D stood nearby, his face a mask of concern.

"O, these Junior Mafia cats ain't playin'. They've been musclin' in on our turf, demanding a cut. Rico's their leader, and he's got a rep for being cold-blooded," Big D said, his voice low.

Omar nodded, his jaw tight. "I know. We can't let them think they can push us around. But we gotta be smart about this. Can't afford a war right now."

Just then, Mona walked into the room, her face pale with worry. She had overheard their conversation, and the anxiety that had been gnawing at her for days finally spilled over. "Omar, what's going on? I keep hearing about these Junior Mafia guys. Are we in danger?"

Omar stood up, crossing the room to take her hands in his. "Baby, it's just business. Don't worry about it. I'll handle it."

Mona's eyes flashed with frustration. "Don't tell me not to worry, Omar. This is our life. If something happens to you..." Her voice trailed off, the fear evident in her eyes.

He pulled her into a hug, his voice soothing. "I know, Mona. But I promise, I'll take care of it. You just focus on keeping things steady at home."

As night fell, Omar and Big D prepared to meet with Rico, the notorious leader of the Junior Mafia. The location was a rundown warehouse on the outskirts of the city, a place where deals were made and lives were often lost. The air was thick with tension as they arrived, the sound of distant sirens echoing in the background.

Rico was waiting for them, flanked by his crew. He was a tall, lean man with cold eyes and a predatory smile. "Omar, Big D, nice of you to join us," he said, his voice dripping with false politeness.

Omar stepped forward, his gaze locked on Rico. "Rico, let's cut to the chase. You've been squeezing my people for money. That stops now."

Rico's smile widened. "Oh, Omar, you misunderstand. This isn't a squeeze. It's an opportunity. We work together, we all get rich. You keep your territory, and I get a small fee for ensuring no one else messes with you."

Omar's eyes narrowed. "And what's to stop me from taking you out right here, right now?"

Rico chuckled, the sound cold and humorless. "Because you know as well as I do, that'll just start a war you can't win. My people are everywhere, and they won't stop until you're done. But if we work together, we can make this city ours."

Omar felt the weight of the decision pressing down on him. He knew Rico was right; a full-blown war would devastate his empire. But giving in to the Junior Mafia's demands would mean losing control. He glanced at Big D, who gave a subtle nod, a sign of trust in Omar's judgment.

"Fine," Omar said finally. "We'll work together. But don't think for a second that means I trust you."

Rico's smile returned. "Trust is earned, Omar. And I'm sure we'll have plenty of time to earn each other's."

The deal was struck, but the tension was far from over. As Omar and Big D drove back through the dark streets, the weight of the decision hung heavy in the air.

Back at home, Mona paced the living room, her anxiety mounting. When Omar finally walked through the door, she rushed to him, her relief palpable. "What happened?"

Omar kissed her forehead, his voice calm. "We came to an agreement. The Junior Mafia won't be a problem, for now."

Mona frowned, sensing the unspoken threat. "But for how long, Omar? How long until they come after us again?"

He sighed, pulling her close. "I don't know, Mona. But we'll deal with it. One step at a time."

The days that followed were tense. Omar's empire was stable, but the threat of the Junior Mafia lingered like a dark cloud. Mona's anxiety grew, the constant fear gnawing at her. She found herself looking over her shoulder, jumping at every unexpected noise.

Tasha, sensing Mona's distress, visited her one afternoon. "Girl, you gotta calm down. You're gonna drive yourself crazy worrying like this."

Mona shook her head, her eyes filled with worry. "I can't help it, Tasha. This life, it's all I know, but it's so dangerous. Every day, I'm scared something will happen to Omar, or to us."

Tasha hugged her friend tightly. "We're gonna get through this, Mona. We always do. You just gotta stay strong."

Meanwhile, Omar's dealings with Rico were tense but steady. The two men maintained a wary truce, each aware that the other could become a deadly enemy at any moment. Omar knew he had to keep his guard up, but the constant pressure was taking its toll.

One evening, as Omar and Mona sat on the couch, the weight of their world pressing down on them, Omar spoke softly. "Mona, I know this isn't the life you wanted. But it's the life we have. And I promise, I'll do everything I can to keep you safe."

Mona looked into his eyes, her heart aching with love and fear. "I just want us to be okay, Omar. I want us to have a future."

He nodded, his resolve hardening. "We will, Mona. We will."

As the city lights flickered outside their window, Omar and Mona held onto each other, finding strength in their love. The Junior Mafia was a looming threat, but they faced it together, determined to survive the dangerous game they were caught in.

Their lives were a delicate balance of luxury and danger, trust and betrayal. In the world they lived in, nothing was guaranteed. But as long as they had each other, they knew they could face whatever came their way. The game was far from over, and the stakes were higher than ever. But Omar and Mona were ready, their love and resilience guiding them through the darkness.

Chapter 4: Love and Loyalty

The love between Mona and Omar was a complicated dance, one that balanced the allure of power with the deep-seated fear of losing everything. In the heart of Norfolk, their relationship was a beacon of resilience amidst chaos, yet it faced strains that threatened to unravel it at the seams.

Omar had always been Mona's anchor, his confidence and ambition drawing her in like a moth to a flame. Their chemistry was undeniable, a magnetic pull that kept them together through thick and thin. But as Omar's empire grew, so did the distance between them. The constant threat of violence and betrayal took its toll, and Mona found herself struggling to keep their love alive.

Mona's days were filled with worry. Every time Omar stepped out the door, she feared he might not come back. She tried to mask her anxiety with shopping trips and spa days, but nothing could erase the gnawing fear that lingered in her heart. She needed him close, but his world was one of danger, and she couldn't change that.

One evening, after a particularly stressful day dealing with the Junior Mafia's demands, Omar returned home late. Mona was waiting for him, her eyes reflecting a mixture of relief and frustration.

"Omar, we need to talk," she said, her voice trembling slightly.

He sighed, running a hand through his hair. "What is it, Mona? I've had a long day."

"I know, but we can't keep going like this. I'm scared all the time, scared of losing you. We need to find a way to make this work, without all the fear," she pleaded.

Omar pulled her into his arms, holding her close. "I know, baby. I know it's hard. But this is the life we chose. I promise, I'll do everything I can to protect you."

Mona wanted to believe him, but the constant danger and Omar's growing distance were hard to ignore. She needed more than promises; she needed action.

As the weeks passed, the strain between them grew. Omar was spending more time away, dealing with the escalating tension with the Junior Mafia. Mona's insecurity deepened when she noticed Omar's wandering eyes. She had seen the way he looked at other women, a look she hadn't seen directed at her in a long time.

The breaking point came one night at a high-end party. The room was filled with the elite of Norfolk's underworld, and the atmosphere was charged with excitement. Mona noticed Omar talking to a stunning woman, her laughter ringing out like a bell. The woman's hand lingered on Omar's arm, and Mona's heart sank.

Later, as they drove home, Mona couldn't hold back her anger. "Who was she, Omar? The woman you were flirting with all night?"

Omar frowned, his eyes fixed on the road. "What are you talking about, Mona? She's nobody."

"Nobody? She didn't look like nobody to me. You were all over her," Mona shot back, her voice rising.

"Jesus, Mona, you're being paranoid. It's just business. Nothing happened," Omar snapped, his patience wearing thin.

Mona felt a wave of betrayal wash over her. "Just business? You think I'm stupid? I've seen the way you look at other women. I'm not blind."

Omar pulled the car over, turning to face her. "Mona, you need to trust me. I'm dealing with a lot right now, and the last thing I need is you doubting me."

Tears filled Mona's eyes. "It's hard to trust you when I feel like I'm losing you. I love you, Omar, but I can't keep living like this."

Omar's expression softened, and he reached out to wipe her tears. "I love you too, Mona. I don't want to lose you either. But you have to understand, this life... it's complicated."

They sat in silence for a moment, the weight of their words hanging in the air. Mona knew their love was real, but the lifestyle they led was tearing them apart.

Back at home, Mona confided in Tasha, her best friend. "I don't know what to do, Tasha. I love Omar, but this life is killing me."

Tasha hugged her tightly. "You have to make a choice, Mona. Either you accept this life and find a way to make it work, or you walk away. But you can't keep torturing yourself like this."

Mona nodded, her mind racing. She knew Tasha was right, but the thought of leaving Omar was too painful to bear. She decided to give their relationship one last chance, hoping they could find a way to make it work.

Omar, too, felt the strain. He loved Mona, but the pressures of his empire were immense. He couldn't afford distractions, and the growing tension between them was becoming just that. He needed to refocus, to remind himself why he started down this path in the first place.

As days turned into weeks, the distance between them grew. Omar's flirtations with other women became more frequent, each one a dagger to Mona's heart. She tried to confront him, but each argument ended the same way: with promises that felt increasingly hollow.

The breaking point came when Mona found a text message on Omar's phone, a message from the woman at the party. The words were innocuous, but the intent was clear. Heartbroken, Mona confronted Omar, the hurt and anger spilling out in a torrent.

"Omar, I found the message. Don't lie to me. You're cheating on me, aren't you?" Mona's voice was raw with emotion.

Omar's face hardened. "Mona, I told you, it's just business. You're blowing this out of proportion."

Mona's tears flowed freely. "No, Omar, you're lying. I can't do this anymore. I need you to choose—me or this life."

Omar's silence was deafening. He looked away, unable to meet her eyes. Mona felt her heart shatter, the last vestiges of her hope crumbling.

With a heavy heart, Mona packed her bags. She couldn't stay and watch their love disintegrate any longer. As she walked out the door, Omar's voice followed her, a whisper filled with regret.

"I'm sorry, Mona."

The door closed behind her, and Mona felt a mix of relief and sorrow. She loved Omar, but she couldn't sacrifice herself for a love that was destroying her. It was time to find a new path, one where she could heal and rebuild.

As she drove away, Mona looked back at the life she was leaving behind. It was filled with love and pain, loyalty and betrayal. But it was time to move forward, to find a new beginning. And as the city lights faded in her rearview mirror, Mona knew she had made the right choice.

Chapter 5: Street Gossip

The sun hung low over Norfolk, casting long shadows across the streets that were alive with whispers and rumors. The talk of the town was Omar and his empire, and the latest gossip was more venomous than ever. From corner stores to barbershops, everyone had something to say about Omar's operations and his wandering eyes.

"Yo, you hear about Omar?" a man whispered to his friend as they leaned against a graffiti-covered wall.

"Yeah, man. Word is he's messin' around on Mona. Ain't no way that's gonna end well," his friend replied, shaking his head.

The rumor mill was relentless, churning out stories that spread like wildfire. Mona heard the whispers too, and each one cut her deeper than the last. She couldn't escape them; they were everywhere, infiltrating her thoughts and her heart.

One evening, as Omar returned home from a late-night meeting, Mona was waiting for him in the living room. Her face was a mask of anger and hurt, her arms crossed tightly over her chest.

"Omar, we need to talk," she said, her voice cold.

Omar sighed, already sensing where this conversation was headed. "What now, Mona?"

"I'm hearing things, Omar. Everyone's talking about you, about us. They're saying you're cheating on me, that your business is falling apart. Is any of it true?" she demanded, her eyes blazing.

Omar's face hardened. "It's just street talk, Mona. People love to gossip. You should know better than to listen to that bullshit."

Mona stepped closer, her voice rising. "Don't you dare dismiss me like that. I'm not some naive girl. I know what's going on. You think I don't see the way you look at other women? The messages on your phone?"

Omar clenched his fists, struggling to keep his temper in check. "I told you, it's just business. You need to trust me."

"Trust you? How can I trust you when everyone's saying the same thing? You're not the man I fell in love with, Omar. You've changed," Mona shot back, her voice trembling with emotion.

The argument escalated, their voices echoing through the house. Omar's frustration boiled over, and he slammed his fist onto the table. "I'm out there every day risking my life to keep us safe, to give us this life. And all you do is doubt me?"

Mona's eyes filled with tears. "I doubt you because you give me reasons to. You're never here, and when you are, you're distant. I can't live like this, Omar."

The tension between them was palpable, the love they once shared now overshadowed by anger and mistrust. Omar stormed out of the house, slamming the door behind him. Mona collapsed onto the couch, her heart heavy with sorrow.

Meanwhile, the streets continued to buzz with gossip, and Big D found himself caught in the middle. As Omar's right-hand man, he was privy to all the secrets and operations, but his loyalty was being tested.

At a local bar, a group of men huddled in a corner, their voices low but intense. "Yo, Big D, you hear what they sayin' about Omar? That he's losin' his grip?"

Big D narrowed his eyes. "People always talk. Omar's got everything under control."

One of the men smirked. "You sure about that? Word is, Junior Mafia's been making moves, and Omar's too busy chasin' tail to notice."

Big D felt his blood boil. "Watch your mouth. Omar's got eyes and ears everywhere. You don't wanna be on his bad side."

But the seed of doubt had been planted, and Big D knew it. The rumors were getting louder, and his loyalty to Omar was being questioned not just by the streets, but by himself. He had always stood by Omar, but the pressure was mounting.

That night, Big D met with Omar in a secluded warehouse, the tension between them palpable. "O, we gotta talk. The streets are buzzin' with rumors. People are starting to doubt you, and that's dangerous."

Omar's eyes flashed with anger. "I know what people are saying. But you need to trust me, D. I've got this under control."

Big D hesitated, the weight of his loyalty heavy on his shoulders. "I trust you, O. But we need to squash these rumors, fast. They're makin' us look weak."

Omar nodded, his expression steely. "We will. But right now, I need you to stay focused. Keep an eye on things and let me handle the rest."

As Big D left the warehouse, he couldn't shake the feeling that things were spiraling out of control. The rumors, the infidelities, the mounting pressure—it was all becoming too much.

Back at home, Mona sat in silence, her mind racing. The love she had for Omar was still there, but it was overshadowed by the pain and betrayal she felt. She needed to make a decision—whether to stay and fight for their relationship or to walk away and protect her heart.

The streets of Norfolk were relentless, their whispers a constant reminder of the danger and deceit that surrounded them. Omar's empire was built on power and fear, but it was crumbling from within. The love and loyalty that had once been their foundation were now being tested like never before.

As the night wore on, Mona made a decision. She would confront Omar one last time, lay everything on the line, and demand the truth. If their love was to survive, they needed to face the rumors head-on and rebuild the trust that had been shattered.

The next morning, as Omar returned home, Mona was waiting for him. Her eyes were resolute, her heart heavy but determined. "Omar, we need to talk. Really talk. No more lies, no more excuses."

Omar looked at her, seeing the pain and determination in her eyes. He knew this was a turning point, a moment that would define their future. He took a deep breath, ready to face the truth, no matter how painful.

"Alright, Mona. Let's talk," he said, his voice steady but filled with emotion.

As they sat down together, the weight of the street gossip and their strained relationship hung over them. But for the first time in a long time, they were ready to confront it together, to find a way through the darkness and rebuild the love and loyalty that had once defined them.

Chapter 6: The Price of Power

The chill of a Norfolk night was cut through by the wail of sirens, but Omar's mind was elsewhere, drowning in the noise of his thoughts. The Junior Mafia was tightening its grip, and the pressure was suffocating. Every move Omar made was watched, every deal scrutinized. It was a game of cat and mouse, and the stakes were higher than ever.

"O, we got a problem," Big D said, his voice urgent as he entered Omar's office. "Junior Mafia's been making moves on our territory again. They took out one of our spots on the east side."

Omar's jaw tightened. "Who was there?"

"Tony and his crew," Big D replied, his expression grim. "Tony didn't make it."

The news hit Omar like a punch to the gut. Tony had been more than just an associate; he was family. The loss was personal and it was a stark reminder of the price they were paying for power.

Omar slammed his fist on the desk, anger boiling over. "We need to hit back, D. We can't let this slide. Rico thinks he can push us around, but he's about to learn a hard lesson."

Big D nodded. "I'm with you, O. But we need to be smart about this. We can't afford to lose more people."

Omar's eyes were steely. "Get the crew together. We're sending a message tonight."

As Omar prepared for the confrontation, Mona sat at home, her anxiety growing with each passing minute. She knew something was wrong; she could feel it in the air. When Omar finally walked through the door, his face was a mask of determination and rage.

"Omar, what's going on? You look like you're about to go to war," Mona said, her voice trembling.

He pulled her into a hug, trying to reassure her. "We lost Tony tonight. The Junior Mafia's getting bold, and we need to remind them who's in charge."

Mona's heart sank. She knew this life was dangerous, but every loss made it more real. "Omar, please be careful. I can't lose you too."

He kissed her forehead. "I'll be fine, Mona. I promise."

But promises in their world were as fragile as glass. Omar left, and Mona was left alone with her fears. She paced the living room, her mind racing with worst-case scenarios. The reality of their dangerous life was hitting her harder than ever, and she didn't know how much more she could take.

Meanwhile, Omar and Big D led their crew to the east side, ready for a showdown. The tension was palpable as they approached one of the Junior Mafia's hangouts. Omar's heart pounded with a mix of anger and adrenaline.

"Remember, we're sending a message," Omar said, his voice low and deadly. "No one disrespects us and gets away with it."

The confrontation was swift and brutal. Gunshots echoed through the night, the air thick with the smell of gunpowder and fear. Omar's men moved with precision, taking down their targets with ruthless efficiency. But the Junior Mafia fought back hard, and the street was soon littered with bodies.

Omar found himself face to face with Rico, the man who had been a thorn in his side for too long. "This is your last chance, Rico," Omar growled. "Back off, or I'll make sure you regret it."

Rico sneered, blood dripping from a cut on his forehead. "You don't scare me, Omar. This city is big enough for both of us, but if you want a war, you got it."

The two men stared each other down, the tension thick enough to cut with a knife. Omar knew this wasn't the end, but a temporary reprieve. The battle lines had been drawn, and the war was far from over.

As Omar returned home, the weight of the night's events pressed heavily on his shoulders. He found Mona waiting for him, her eyes filled with worry and fear. "What happened?" she asked, her voice barely above a whisper.

"We hit them hard. Sent a message. But this isn't over, Mona. Rico's not backing down," Omar said, his voice grim.

Mona's heart ached. "Omar, I'm scared. Every time you walk out that door, I'm scared you won't come back."

He took her hands, his gaze intense. "I know, Mona. But this is the life we chose. I need you to be strong, for both of us."

She nodded, tears filling her eyes. "I'll try, Omar. But it's so hard."

The price of power was steep, and they were both paying it. Omar's empire was under constant threat, and the toll it was taking on their relationship was becoming more evident with each passing day.

In the days that followed, the streets buzzed with the aftermath of the confrontation. The Junior Mafia was licking its wounds, but Omar knew they would be back, more determined than ever. The cycle of violence and retribution seemed endless, and each victory was bittersweet.

Mona tried to find solace in the small moments of peace they shared, but the fear never truly left her. She watched Omar closely, seeing the toll the constant pressure was taking on him. The man she loved was changing, hardened by the relentless demands of their world.

One evening, as they sat together in the quiet of their home, Mona voiced her deepest fears. "Omar, what if it never ends? What if this is our life forever, always looking over our shoulders, always fighting to stay on top?"

Omar looked at her, his eyes weary but determined. "I don't know, Mona. But as long as we're together, I'll keep fighting. For us, for our future."

His words were meant to reassure, but Mona couldn't shake the feeling that their future was as uncertain as ever. The price of power was a heavy burden, and they were both struggling under its weight.

As the city settled into an uneasy calm, Omar and Mona held each other close, finding strength in their love even as the world around them threatened to tear them apart. The road ahead was fraught with danger, but they faced it together, their bond a beacon of hope in the darkness.

The price of power had claimed its first major loss, and the reality of their dangerous life was clearer than ever. But Omar and Mona were determined to weather the storm, to find a way through the chaos and build a future together, no matter the cost.

Chapter 7: Trust and Betrayal

The streets of Norfolk were no place for the weak. Trust was a rare commodity, and betrayal lurked around every corner. Omar had built his empire on loyalty, but even the strongest foundations could be shaken. The revelation of Big D's betrayal would turn Omar's world upside down, pushing him to the edge of paranoia and forcing Mona to step up in ways she never imagined.

The whispers started small, barely more than a murmur on the streets. But as the days passed, they grew louder, more insistent. Omar heard them everywhere he went, the same words repeating like a sinister mantra: Big D was working with the Junior Mafia.

Omar tried to dismiss the rumors at first, trusting in the loyalty of his right-hand man. But as the evidence mounted, doubt began to creep in. Big D's recent actions had been questionable, his loyalty appearing more and more suspect. The seed of paranoia was planted, and it took root deep in Omar's mind.

One evening, after another tense meeting, Omar confronted Big D in the dimly lit confines of his office. The air was thick with tension, the unspoken accusations hanging between them like a storm cloud.

"D, we need to talk," Omar said, his voice low and dangerous.

Big D leaned back in his chair, his eyes narrowing. "What's up, O? You look like you've seen a ghost."

Omar's jaw clenched. "I've been hearing things. People are saying you're working with the Junior Mafia. That you've been feeding them information."

Big D's face twisted in anger. "What the fuck are you talking about, Omar? You think I'd betray you after everything we've been through?"

Omar stepped closer, his eyes blazing. "I don't want to believe it, D. But too many things aren't adding up. I need the truth."

Big D stood, his fists clenched. "The truth is, I've been loyal to you from day one. If you're gonna let some street gossip get between us, then maybe you don't know me as well as you think."

The tension in the room was palpable, the air crackling with the threat of violence. Omar's paranoia had reached a boiling point, and he could no longer ignore the possibility of betrayal. He drew his gun, pointing it at Big D.

"Don't make me do this, D. Tell me the truth," Omar demanded, his voice shaking with a mix of anger and desperation.

Big D's eyes flashed with defiance. "You're making a big mistake, O. But if you're gonna pull that trigger, you better be damn sure."

For a moment, time seemed to stand still. Omar's finger hovered over the trigger, his mind racing with doubt and fear. He didn't want to believe that his closest ally could betray him, but the paranoia was too strong to ignore.

Before he could make a decision, the door to the office burst open, and Mona rushed in. She had overheard their argument, her heart pounding with fear. "Omar, stop! You can't do this!"

Omar turned to her, his eyes wild. "Mona, stay out of this. This is between me and D."

"No, Omar. This affects all of us. If you kill him, you'll be doing exactly what the Junior Mafia wants. We need to be smarter than this," Mona pleaded, her voice shaking.

Big D lowered his fists, his expression softening slightly. "Listen to her, O. Don't let them tear us apart from the inside."

Omar's grip on the gun loosened, his mind torn between trust and betrayal. With a deep breath, he lowered the weapon, his eyes still locked on Big D. "This isn't over, D. But for now, we'll figure this out together."

As the tension eased, the three of them sat down, trying to piece together the truth. Mona's role in Omar's empire became more critical than ever as she helped navigate the fallout of the betrayal. She worked tirelessly to gather information, reaching out to their network and trying to identify the true traitor.

The days that followed were fraught with tension and uncertainty. Omar's paranoia grew, his trust in those around him eroded by the constant threat of betrayal. He relied heavily on Mona, her steady presence a lifeline in the chaos.

Mona, for her part, found herself stepping into a role she had never anticipated. She became Omar's confidante and advisor, her insights crucial in navigating the treacherous waters of their world. Her fear for Omar's safety drove her to be more involved, her love for him pushing her to fight harder than ever.

One night, as they sat together in the quiet of their home, Omar spoke softly. "Mona, I don't know what I'd do without you. You've been my rock through all of this."

She looked at him, her eyes filled with determination. "We're in this together, Omar. No matter what happens, we'll face it as a team."

Their bond was tested, but it held strong. As they navigated the aftermath of Big D's betrayal, they grew closer, their love and loyalty a beacon of hope in the darkness.

In the end, the true traitor was revealed to be another associate, using Big D as a scapegoat to cover his tracks. The revelation brought a sense of relief, but the damage had been done. Trust was a fragile thing, and it would take time to rebuild.

Omar and Mona faced the future with a renewed sense of purpose, their resolve stronger than ever. The streets of Norfolk were unforgiving, but together, they were a force to be reckoned with. The price of power was steep, but their love and loyalty gave them the strength to pay it.

As they stood together, ready to face whatever challenges lay ahead, they knew one thing for certain: they would always have each other's backs, no matter the cost. The game was far from over, but they were ready to play it to win.

Chapter 8: The Highs and Lows

The sun had barely risen over Norfolk when Omar sealed the deal that would change everything. It was a major score, a shipment of pure product that would flood the streets and fill his coffers. For the first time in months, the weight on his shoulders lifted slightly. The tension that had plagued him, the paranoia that had driven a wedge between him and his closest allies, eased—if only for a moment.

Omar strolled into their lavish home, his grin as bright as the morning light spilling through the windows. Mona was in the kitchen, sipping her coffee and flipping through a magazine. She looked up as he entered, immediately sensing his elation.

"We did it, Mona. The biggest deal yet," he said, pulling her into an embrace.

She smiled, but there was a shadow behind her eyes. "That's great, Omar. I'm happy for you."

He noticed the hesitation in her voice, but chose to ignore it. "Let's celebrate. Tonight, we hit the town, show this city what we're made of."

The night arrived, and Omar and Mona stepped out in style. They drove through the city in Omar's latest acquisition, a sleek black Lamborghini that turned heads wherever it went. The club was one of the most exclusive in Norfolk, and they were treated like royalty. Bottles of champagne flowed, and the music pulsed through the floor, a heartbeat of their triumph.

Mona tried to lose herself in the celebration, to let the music and the luxury drown out her doubts. She clung to Omar, her lifeline in this turbulent sea. But as she looked around at the opulence and the dangerous men who shared their world, her mind was a storm of conflicting emotions.

"Look at you, girl! Living the dream," Tasha shouted over the music, her eyes sparkling with excitement.

Mona forced a smile. "Yeah, Tasha. Living the dream."

But was it her dream? Or was it a nightmare she couldn't wake from? The money, the power, the endless parties—it was a seductive life, but it came with a price. Every moment of joy was shadowed by the threat of violence, the constant danger that lurked around every corner.

As the night wore on, Omar and Mona returned home, their laughter echoing through the halls. But as soon as the door closed behind them, the weight of their reality settled back in. Mona watched Omar as he moved through their luxurious home, a king surveying his kingdom. She loved him deeply, but she couldn't shake the feeling that their life was built on a foundation of sand.

"Omar, can we talk?" she asked, her voice softer now.

He turned to her, sensing the shift in her tone. "What's on your mind, Mona?"

She took a deep breath, trying to find the right words. "I'm happy for you, for us. But I can't help feeling like... like we're living on borrowed time. This life, it's so dangerous. I'm scared, Omar. Every day, I'm scared."

He sighed, walking over to her and taking her hands. "I know, Mona. But this is the life we chose. We've worked too hard to give it up now. And I promise, I'll keep you safe."

Mona's eyes filled with tears. "I don't doubt your love, Omar. But sometimes I wonder if it's worth it. The money, the power—it's not worth losing you."

Omar pulled her close, kissing her forehead. "We're in this together, Mona. We've got each other, and that's all that matters. We just need to stay strong."

She nodded, but the doubts remained. Her dependency on Omar's wealth and power was a gilded cage, trapping her in a life she wasn't sure she wanted. The highs of their success were exhilarating, but the lows were devastating, and the fear of losing everything was always present.

The next few weeks were a blur of business and pleasure. Omar's deal had temporarily eased the pressure, and they enjoyed the fruits of their labor. Lavish dinners, designer clothes, and extravagant gifts filled their days. But Mona's internal conflict grew with each passing moment.

She watched Omar as he navigated their dangerous world, admired his strength and determination. But she couldn't shake the feeling that they were on a precipice, teetering on the edge of disaster. The threat of violence was a constant shadow, a reminder that their world could crumble in an instant.

One evening, as they sat together on their balcony, overlooking the city lights, Mona spoke the thoughts that had been haunting her. "Omar, do you ever think about leaving? About finding a way out?"

He looked at her, surprised. "Leaving? Mona, this is our life. We've built something here."

"I know. But what if we could build something different? Something safer?" she asked, her voice trembling.

Omar's expression softened, and he took her hand. "I've thought about it. But the streets don't let go that easily. We're in deep, Mona. And I don't know if there's a way out."

She squeezed his hand, her heart heavy with the weight of their reality. "I just want us to be happy, Omar. I want us to be safe."

"We'll find a way, Mona. I promise," he said, but the uncertainty in his voice was unmistakable.

As they sat together, the city sprawled out before them, they both knew the truth. Their life was a delicate balance of highs and lows, a dance with danger that could end at any moment. But for now, they had each other, and that was enough to keep them going.

The highs of their success were sweet, but the lows were a stark reminder of the price they paid. Mona's internal conflict was far from resolved, but her love for Omar gave her the strength to face each day. Together, they would navigate the treacherous waters of their world, holding onto the hope that they could find a way to build a future free from fear.

Chapter 9: The Fall of Allies

The streets of Norfolk were buzzing with tension, a storm brewing just below the surface. For Omar and Mona, the illusion of stability they had recently enjoyed was about to be shattered. The fall of allies began with Tasha, Mona's best friend, whose involvement in the drug game brought unforeseen trouble.

Tasha had always been a force to be reckoned with, her confidence and street smarts making her a valuable asset. But as the stakes grew higher, so did the risks. Omar had warned her to stay low, but Tasha's ambitions had led her into deeper waters. She had started running small deals on the side, hoping to make a name for herself.

One evening, Mona received a frantic call from Tasha. "Mona, you gotta help me. The cops are all over me. They're saying I'm going down for distribution. I don't know what to do!"

Mona's heart sank. "Where are you, Tasha?"

"I'm at the corner of Elm and 5th. Please, Mona, I need you."

Mona grabbed her keys and rushed out the door, her mind racing. She knew the consequences of Tasha's actions, and the fear that gripped her was almost paralyzing. When she arrived at the scene, it was already swarming with police. Tasha was in handcuffs, her face a mask of fear and defiance.

"Tasha!" Mona shouted, pushing through the crowd. "What happened?"

Tasha's eyes filled with tears. "They found the stash, Mona. Someone must have tipped them off. I'm done for."

Mona's mind reeled. She knew she had to act fast. She called Omar, her voice shaking. "Omar, it's Tasha. She's been arrested. They found drugs on her."

Omar's voice was grim. "I told her to stay out of it. Damn it. I'll see what I can do, but this is bad, Mona. Real bad."

As Tasha was taken away, Mona felt a crushing sense of helplessness. She had always been loyal to her friend, but now that loyalty was being tested in ways she had never imagined. The fear for her own safety and the safety of Omar weighed heavily on her.

Back at home, Omar was pacing the floor, his frustration evident. "Tasha should have listened. Now we're all at risk. The cops are going to be all over us."

Mona's eyes were filled with tears. "She's my best friend, Omar. We can't just abandon her."

"I'm not saying we abandon her, Mona. But we need to be smart about this. We can't let this bring us down too," Omar said, his voice softening as he pulled her into a hug.

The days that followed were a blur of legal battles and growing tension. Mona visited Tasha in jail, her heart breaking at the sight of her friend behind bars. "We're going to get you out of here, Tasha. I promise."

Tasha shook her head, her eyes filled with despair. "I don't know, Mona. They're saying I'm looking at ten years. I don't know if I can survive that."

Mona fought back tears. "You're strong, Tasha. We'll find a way."

Meanwhile, Omar's empire was under siege. The police crackdown that had caught Tasha wasn't an isolated incident. More of Omar's associates were being taken out or arrested, and the pressure was mounting. His business was suffering, and the sense of control he had fought so hard to maintain was slipping through his fingers.

Omar sat in a meeting with his remaining crew, the tension thick in the air. "We need to tighten up. No more mistakes. The cops are breathing down our necks, and we can't afford any more losses."

Big D nodded, his expression grim. "We're already down two more guys. This isn't just a crackdown, O. Someone's feeding them information."

Omar's eyes narrowed. "Then we find out who. And we deal with them."

As the meeting broke up, Omar felt the weight of their situation pressing down on him. He returned home, finding Mona in the living room, her face pale with worry.

"How's Tasha?" he asked, sitting beside her.

"Scared. They're throwing everything at her, Omar. I don't know how much more she can take," Mona said, her voice trembling.

Omar took her hand, his eyes filled with determination. "We'll get her the best lawyer. We'll fight this. But we need to stay strong, Mona. For her, and for us."

Mona nodded, her heart heavy with the burden of their reality. The fall of their allies was a stark reminder of the precariousness of their world. Every move they made was fraught with danger, every decision a potential tipping point.

That night, as they lay in bed, Mona couldn't shake the fear that gripped her. "Omar, what if we're next? What if everything we've built comes crashing down?"

Omar pulled her close, his voice a soothing whisper. "We won't let that happen, Mona. We'll fight for what's ours. No matter what."

The words were meant to comfort, but the uncertainty lingered. Mona knew that the fight was far from over, and the price they paid for power was steep. As the shadows of their world closed in, they held onto each other, finding strength in their love and loyalty.

The fall of their allies was a blow, but it was not the end. Omar and Mona were determined to rise above the chaos, to protect their empire and those they cared about. The road ahead was fraught with peril, but they faced it together, their bond unbreakable in the face of adversity.

Chapter 10: Baby Mama Drama

The streets of Norfolk were never silent, always alive with whispers and secrets that cut deeper than any blade. Omar and Mona were no strangers to scandal, but the latest revelation hit closer to home than any street rumor. Omar's past had come back to haunt him, and it brought a whirlwind of drama that threatened to tear their world apart.

It all began on an otherwise ordinary afternoon. Omar was in his office, going over plans to secure his operations after the recent police crackdowns, when his phone buzzed. The message was simple, but the impact was explosive: "Omar, we need to talk. It's about your son. – Tiana."

Omar's heart skipped a beat. Tiana was an old flame, a chapter of his life he thought he had closed. The last he'd heard, she had moved to another city, far away from the chaos of Norfolk. He tried to push the thoughts aside, but the implications gnawed at him.

When Mona came home that evening, she immediately sensed something was wrong. Omar's usually composed demeanor was fractured, and she saw the tension in his eyes.

"What's going on, Omar?" Mona asked, her voice steady but filled with concern.

He sighed, rubbing his temples. "We need to talk, Mona. There's something you need to know."

Mona's heart raced, her mind jumping to the worst conclusions. "Just tell me, Omar. Don't drag it out."

"Tiana's back in town. She's saying I have a son. That he's mine," Omar said, his voice low and filled with regret.

Mona's eyes widened, a storm of emotions swirling within her. "What the fuck, Omar? How could you keep this from me?"

"I didn't know, Mona. I swear. She just reached out today. I had no idea," he pleaded, trying to reach for her.

Mona recoiled, her anger flaring. "You expect me to believe that? You've been lying to me all this time?"

Omar stood up, frustration boiling over. "I haven't been lying, Mona. This is just as much a shock to me as it is to you."

"Do you have any idea what this does to us? To me?" Mona shouted, tears streaming down her face. "I've stood by you through everything, and now this?"

Omar's heart ached seeing her in pain, but he knew there was no easy way to fix this. "I'm sorry, Mona. I don't know what else to say."

She turned away, trying to gather her thoughts. The betrayal she felt was overwhelming, and the scandal was sure to be the talk of the streets. Their relationship had been strained already, and this revelation felt like the final blow.

As the news spread, the streets buzzed with gossip. Omar's enemies reveled in the scandal, using it as ammunition to undermine his authority. Friends and allies questioned his loyalty and integrity. The whispers were relentless, each one chipping away at the foundation of Omar and Mona's life.

"Yo, you hear about Omar? Got himself a baby mama drama now," one man said to his friend at a local bar.

"Yeah, man. Wonder how Mona's taking it. Can't be easy knowing your man's got another kid out there," his friend replied, shaking his head.

The scandal became the topic of every conversation, further complicating their lives. Omar tried to maintain control over his empire, but the constant distraction of Tiana and the child weighed heavily on him. He met with Tiana, demanding answers.

"Tiana, why now? Why come to me after all these years?" Omar asked, his frustration barely contained.

Tiana sighed, her expression weary. "I didn't know how to find you, Omar. I didn't want to disrupt your life. But our son deserves to know his father."

Omar felt a pang of guilt and anger. "You should have come to me sooner. This mess could have been avoided."

"I'm here now, Omar. That's all that matters," Tiana said softly. "I'm not here to cause trouble. I just want what's best for our son."

Meanwhile, Mona struggled with her own emotions. She loved Omar, but the betrayal cut deep. The scandal and the constant buzz of the streets added to her turmoil. She confided in Tasha, who was still dealing with her own legal troubles.

"Mona, you gotta stay strong. This is just another test," Tasha said, her voice firm. "You've been through worse. You can get through this too."

Mona nodded, but the pain was evident in her eyes. "I just don't know if I can trust him anymore, Tasha. Everything feels like it's falling apart."

"You and Omar have something real. Don't let this tear you apart. Fight for it," Tasha encouraged, squeezing her friend's hand.

As days turned into weeks, Omar and Mona's relationship remained strained. Omar tried to make amends, spending more time with Mona and proving his commitment. But the shadow of Tiana and the child loomed large.

One evening, as they sat in their living room, Omar reached for Mona's hand. "Mona, I know I've messed up. But I'm trying to make things right. Can we get through this together?"

Mona looked into his eyes, searching for the sincerity she needed to see. "I don't know, Omar. This is a lot to take in. But I do know I love you. And maybe that's a start."

Their journey was far from over, and the road ahead was fraught with challenges. The baby mama drama had rocked their world, but it hadn't destroyed them. As they navigated the complexities of their relationship and the ever-watchful eyes of the streets, they held onto the hope that love and loyalty would see them through.

The scandal might have shaken their foundation, but it also gave them a chance to rebuild stronger than before. Together, they faced the future, determined to overcome the highs and lows that life threw their way. The streets of Norfolk were unforgiving, but Omar and Mona were ready to fight for their love and their empire, no matter the cost.

Chapter 11: The Art of Extortion

The Junior Mafia was a relentless force, and their latest moves showed they were not backing down. They had shifted their strategy, no longer content to simply disrupt Omar's operations. Now, they were targeting his heart: Mona. The art of extortion was their game, and they played it with brutal efficiency.

One evening, as Mona was closing up the boutique she managed, she noticed a black SUV parked across the street. It had been there for hours, its tinted windows hiding whoever was inside. She felt a shiver of unease but brushed it off, chalking it up to paranoia. As she locked the door and started walking to her car, the SUV's engine roared to life. Her heart pounded as it slowly rolled up beside her.

The window rolled down, and a menacing face appeared. "Evening, Mona. We need to talk," the man said, his voice cold and menacing.

Mona's blood ran cold. She recognized him instantly – Rico, the leader of the Junior Mafia. "What do you want, Rico?" she asked, trying to keep her voice steady.

He smirked, leaning out the window. "It's simple. We want what's ours. Omar's been holding out on us, and you're gonna help us fix that."

"I don't know what you're talking about," Mona replied, taking a step back.

Rico's smile vanished. "Don't play dumb, Mona. You know exactly what we want. Tell Omar to pay up, or things are gonna get real ugly for you."

Before she could respond, Rico's hand shot out, grabbing her wrist. The sudden violence shocked her, but she fought to keep her composure. "Let go of me, Rico," she hissed, her eyes blazing with anger.

He tightened his grip, his eyes cold. "You tell Omar he's got one week to come up with the money. One week, Mona. After that, we come for you."

With that, he released her and the SUV sped away, leaving Mona trembling with fear and rage. She hurried to her car, her mind racing. She had to tell Omar, but she knew this would escalate things to a dangerous level.

When she arrived home, Omar was waiting for her. The moment he saw her face, he knew something was wrong. "Mona, what happened?" he asked, his voice filled with concern.

She took a deep breath, trying to steady herself. "Rico. He cornered me outside the shop. He's demanding money, Omar. He said if you don't pay, they're coming for me."

Omar's expression darkened, his anger simmering just beneath the surface. "That son of a bitch. I'll kill him."

Mona grabbed his arm, her eyes pleading. "Omar, please. We need to be smart about this. I don't want you getting hurt."

He pulled her into a tight embrace, his mind racing with how to protect her and maintain his grip on his empire. "I'll handle this, Mona. I promise. They won't touch you."

The next few days were a blur of tension and fear. Omar intensified his security measures, placing guards around their home and Mona's boutique. But the threat of the Junior Mafia was a constant shadow, hanging over them like a dark cloud.

Mona tried to go about her daily life, but the fear was always there. She felt it in every glance from a stranger, every unexpected noise. Her bravery was put to the test as she faced the reality of their dangerous world.

One afternoon, as she was leaving the boutique, she saw a group of men approaching. Her heart raced, but she held her ground. "What do you want?" she demanded, her voice steady despite her fear.

The leader of the group sneered. "Just a message for your boyfriend. Time's running out."

Before she could react, he shoved her against the wall, his grip bruising her arm. "Tell Omar he's got one day left," he growled, before releasing her and walking away.

Shaken but determined, Mona hurried home. She found Omar in his office, surrounded by his men. "Omar, they came again. They said you've got one day left."

Omar's face hardened. "That's it. We're going to end this, once and for all."

He gathered his crew, laying out a plan to confront the Junior Mafia. "We hit them hard, and we hit them fast. They think they can scare us, but they have no idea who they're dealing with."

Mona watched, her heart heavy with fear and worry. She knew this confrontation was inevitable, but it didn't make it any easier. As Omar prepared to leave, she pulled him aside.

"Please be careful, Omar. I can't lose you," she whispered, tears in her eyes.

He kissed her gently, his gaze intense. "I'll come back to you, Mona. I promise."

The night was dark and silent as Omar and his crew approached the Junior Mafia's hideout. The tension was palpable, every man on edge, knowing what was at stake.

The confrontation was brutal and swift. Gunshots echoed through the night, the air thick with the smell of gunpowder and blood. Omar fought with a fierce determination, driven by the need to protect Mona and his empire.

When the dust settled, Rico lay on the ground, defeated but not dead. Omar stood over him, his gun trained on Rico's head. "This ends now. You come near Mona again, and I will kill you. Do you understand?"

Rico nodded, fear in his eyes. "I get it, Omar. It's over."

Omar lowered his gun, his victory bittersweet. The battle was won, but the war was far from over. As he returned home to Mona, he knew they would face many more challenges, but their love and determination would see them through.

Mona's bravery had been tested, and she had emerged stronger. The threat of violence still loomed, but together, they faced the darkness, ready to protect what was theirs. The streets of Norfolk were unforgiving, but Omar and Mona were determined to survive, no matter the cost.

Chapter 12: Long Prison Sentences

The streets of Norfolk were always simmering with tension, but now they were boiling over. The police had intensified their crackdown on Omar's operations, and the legal heat was turning into a full-blown inferno. Omar's empire, built on the delicate balance of power and secrecy, was starting to crumble, and the fallout was devastating.

It began with a series of coordinated raids. Omar's trusted associates were being picked off one by one, caught in the dragnet of a massive law enforcement operation. The first to fall was Luis, a loyal lieutenant who had been with Omar since the beginning. The charges were severe: drug trafficking, conspiracy, and racketeering. The sentence was even worse: twenty years without parole.

The news hit Omar like a sledgehammer. He had known Luis's arrest was a possibility, but the reality was far harsher than he had imagined. He gathered his remaining crew, their faces grim with the knowledge that they were next in line.

"We've got to be smarter," Omar said, his voice tight with determination. "They're coming for us, but we can't let them take us all down."

Big D nodded, his expression serious. "We need to tighten our circle. No more loose ends."

But even as they planned their next moves, the police were closing in. The next arrest came just days later, and it was a blow that rocked Omar to his core. Rico, a key player in the Junior Mafia who had reluctantly become an ally, was taken down in a sting operation. His sentence was equally severe, and the message was clear: no one was safe.

The streets buzzed with the news, and fear spread like wildfire. Mona could feel the tension in every interaction, every glance. She knew the walls were closing in, and her fear of losing everything was becoming a harsh reality. She watched Omar grow more distant, his mind consumed with trying to save what was left of his empire.

One evening, as they sat in their living room, the weight of their situation pressed down on them. Omar was staring at the TV, but his mind was elsewhere. Mona reached out, taking his hand.

"Omar, we need to talk. This can't go on. We're losing everything," she said, her voice trembling.

He turned to her, his eyes filled with frustration and sadness. "I know, Mona. I'm doing everything I can, but it feels like we're fighting a losing battle."

She squeezed his hand, her own fear mirrored in his eyes. "What are we going to do?"

"I don't know," he admitted, his voice barely above a whisper. "But we can't give up. Not now."

As the days turned into weeks, the arrests continued. Omar's circle grew smaller, each loss a brutal reminder of their vulnerability. The police were relentless, and the sentences handed down were long and unforgiving. Omar's best friend and confidant, Big D, was caught in a sting operation and sentenced to fifteen years. The blow was almost too much for Omar to bear.

Mona's fear grew with each passing day. She watched as the life they had built crumbled around them, the future they had dreamed of slipping through their fingers. She tried to stay strong for Omar, but the fear of losing everything was overwhelming.

One night, as they lay in bed, the weight of their situation pressing down on them, Mona couldn't hold back her tears. "Omar, what if you're next? What if they come for you?"

He pulled her close, his own fear mirrored in her eyes. "We have to keep fighting, Mona. We can't let them win."

But even as he said the words, he knew the odds were against them. The legal heat was relentless, and the cracks in their empire were widening. Mona's fear of losing everything was becoming a harsh reality, and there was little they could do to stop it.

The next morning, the news came that Omar had been dreading. The police had issued a warrant for his arrest. The charges were severe, and the sentence, if convicted, would be long and unforgiving. Mona's heart shattered as the reality of their situation hit her.

"Omar, what are we going to do?" she asked, her voice shaking with fear.

He took a deep breath, his mind racing. "I'm going to turn myself in. It's the only way to protect you."

"No, Omar. You can't," she cried, her fear turning to desperation.

"I have to, Mona. It's the only way to keep you safe," he said, his voice steady but filled with sorrow.

As he prepared to leave, Mona clung to him, tears streaming down her face. "I love you, Omar. Please come back to me."

He kissed her gently, his heart breaking. "I love you too, Mona. And I promise, I'll come back to you."

The walk to the police station was the longest of Omar's life. Each step felt like a step towards an uncertain future, one that might tear him away from the woman he loved and the life they had built together. The streets of Norfolk were cold and unforgiving, but Omar's resolve was strong. He would face whatever came his way, for Mona's sake and for his own.

As he entered the station, the reality of his situation hit him hard. The legal battle ahead would be long and grueling, but Omar was determined to fight. For Mona, for their future, and for the empire he had built.

The price of power was steep, but Omar was willing to pay it. As he was led away in handcuffs, he looked back one last time, his heart filled with determination. He would return to Mona, no matter what it took.

For now, the battle was just beginning.

Chapter 13: Murder and Mayhem

The streets of Norfolk were no stranger to violence, but tonight, they would witness a bloodbath. The tension between Omar's crew and the Junior Mafia had reached a boiling point, and the resulting confrontation would leave the city reeling.

Omar, now out on bail thanks to a high-priced lawyer, was desperately trying to maintain control of his crumbling empire. The arrests and long prison sentences had weakened his grip, but the Junior Mafia's relentless push for dominance threatened to destroy everything. He gathered his remaining crew, their faces a mix of determination and fear.

"We can't let them win," Omar said, his voice low and filled with urgency. "Tonight, we send a message. They want a war, they've got one."

Big D, recently released on bail himself, nodded. "We hit them where it hurts, O. But we gotta be smart. This ain't just about us anymore. It's about survival."

As night fell, the city's shadows seemed to grow darker, the air thick with anticipation. Omar's crew moved through the streets with purpose, their destination a known Junior Mafia stronghold. The plan was simple: hit hard, hit fast, and leave a mark.

Mona, aware of the impending confrontation, was sick with worry. She had tried to convince Omar to find another way, but his resolve was unshakable. She watched from their home, her heart pounding with every passing minute, praying he would come back to her.

The first shots rang out, shattering the night's silence. Omar's crew descended upon the stronghold with a fury, guns blazing. The Junior Mafia was ready, their own weapons drawn, and the two sides clashed in a violent storm of bullets and blood.

Omar moved with precision, his years in the game giving him an edge. But the Junior Mafia was equally ruthless, and the air was soon filled with the sounds of screams and gunfire. Bodies fell on both sides, the ground slick with blood.

Big D fought beside Omar, his loyalty unwavering. But as the battle raged on, a bullet found its mark, and Big D went down. Omar's heart clenched as he saw his friend fall, but there was no time to grieve. He continued to fight, driven by a desperate need to survive.

In the chaos, Omar found himself face-to-face with Rico, the leader of the Junior Mafia. The two men locked eyes, hatred and determination burning between them. Without a word, they lunged at each other, fists flying.

The fight was brutal, each man giving as good as he got. But Omar was fueled by a rage that burned deep, and he finally managed to overpower Rico, slamming him to the ground.

"It's over, Rico," Omar growled, his voice thick with emotion. "This ends now."

Rico spat blood, his eyes defiant even in defeat. "This ain't over, Omar. It's never over."

As the last of the gunfire died down, the aftermath was a scene of carnage. Omar's crew had taken heavy losses, many of his closest allies lying lifeless on the ground. The Junior Mafia was decimated, but the victory felt hollow. The cost had been too high.

Omar stood amidst the wreckage, his body battered and bloodied. The weight of the violence and loss pressed down on him, and a sense of doom settled in his chest. The cycle of violence had escalated, and he knew there would be no end to it.

He returned home in the early hours of the morning, his steps heavy with exhaustion and sorrow. Mona was waiting for him, her face pale and drawn. She rushed to him, her eyes wide with fear and relief.

"Omar, are you okay?" she whispered, her hands trembling as she touched his bruised face.

He nodded, pulling her into a tight embrace. "I'm here, Mona. I'm here."

But even as he held her, the reality of their situation was clear. The violence and bloodshed had taken a toll, and the future was uncertain. The city's underworld was in chaos, and the threat of retaliation loomed large.

In the days that followed, the streets buzzed with the news of the confrontation. The cycle of violence showed no signs of stopping, and the sense of doom grew stronger. Omar's crew was fractured, their numbers dwindling, and the Junior Mafia was licking its wounds, ready to strike back.

Mona watched as Omar struggled to keep control, the weight of their world pressing down on him. She knew they were fighting a losing battle, but she couldn't bear the thought of giving up. They had come too far, sacrificed too much.

One evening, as they sat in their living room, the silence between them was heavy with unspoken fears. Omar finally broke the silence, his voice barely above a whisper.

"Mona, I don't know how much more of this I can take. We're losing everything."

She reached for his hand, her eyes filled with determination. "We can't give up, Omar. We have to find a way out of this. Together."

He looked at her, his heart aching with the love and fear he felt. "I don't know if there is a way out, Mona. But I'll keep fighting for us. For you."

The battle was far from over, and the road ahead was fraught with danger. But Omar and Mona faced it together, their bond a beacon of hope in the darkness. The cycle of violence might seem endless, but their love and determination gave them the strength to keep fighting, no matter the cost.

Chapter 14: The Final Betrayal

The streets of Norfolk had always been a battleground, but the stakes had never been higher. Omar was at his wit's end, struggling to maintain control over his crumbling empire. The cycle of violence and betrayal had left him weary and paranoid, but nothing could have prepared him for the final, most devastating betrayal.

It started with whispers, as it always did. Omar had suspected for weeks that there was a mole within his operation, feeding information to the Junior Mafia and the police. The raids, the arrests, the constant setbacks—someone had to be behind it. Someone close. His heart sank as he realized the implications, the faces of his trusted allies flashing through his mind.

One evening, as Omar sat in his office, poring over ledgers and phone records, he found it: a discrepancy in the numbers, a trail leading back to someone he had never doubted. Carlos, a trusted lieutenant, someone he had considered family. The betrayal hit him like a punch to the gut, leaving him breathless with rage and sorrow.

Omar called a meeting, his face a mask of fury. The remaining members of his crew gathered, their expressions tense and wary. Carlos stood among them, his face carefully neutral.

"We've got a rat in our midst," Omar said, his voice cold and hard. "And I'm going to find out who it is."

He paced the room, his eyes scanning each face, looking for signs of guilt. Finally, he stopped in front of Carlos, his eyes burning with intensity. "Carlos, I need you to explain these numbers."

Carlos's face paled, his eyes darting nervously. "Omar, I—"

Before he could finish, Omar grabbed him by the collar, slamming him against the wall. "You've been selling us out, haven't you? Feeding information to the Junior Mafia? To the cops?"

Carlos's eyes filled with fear and guilt. "Omar, I had no choice! They threatened my family! I didn't want to, but they left me no choice!"

Omar's fury boiled over. "You betrayed us, Carlos! You betrayed me!"

Carlos struggled, but Omar's grip was like iron. The other members of the crew looked on, their faces a mix of anger and betrayal. "Please, Omar, I'm sorry," Carlos pleaded, his voice shaking.

But it was too late. The damage had been done. With a final, rage-filled cry, Omar pulled out his gun and shot Carlos. The sound echoed through the room, a grim punctuation to the betrayal that had shattered their trust.

As the body hit the floor, the reality of the situation sank in. Omar's hands shook, the weight of his actions pressing down on him. He turned to his crew, their faces grim and silent. "We clean this up. Now."

The rest of the night was a blur of activity. The crew worked silently, their movements efficient and practiced. But the sense of camaraderie was gone, replaced by a heavy, oppressive silence.

Mona was waiting for Omar when he returned home, her heart heavy with worry. She had sensed the tension, the growing paranoia, and it had left her anxious and afraid. When she saw the look on Omar's face, her heart sank.

"What happened?" she asked, her voice trembling.

Omar sank into a chair, his face in his hands. "Carlos. He was the mole. I had to... I had to take care of it."

Mona's heart broke as she saw the pain in his eyes. "Omar, this is tearing us apart. The betrayals, the violence... I don't know how much more we can take."

He looked up at her, his eyes filled with sorrow and regret. "I'm trying, Mona. I'm trying to hold everything together, but it feels like everything is slipping away."

She knelt beside him, taking his hands in hers. "I love you, Omar. But this life... it's destroying us. We need to find a way out, before it's too late."

Omar's grip tightened on her hands. "I know, Mona. I know. But I don't know how. Every time I think we're making progress, something else happens. I'm so tired."

The weight of their reality pressed down on them, the constant threat of violence and betrayal leaving them exhausted and broken. The final betrayal had taken a toll, and their relationship was at a breaking point.

As they sat in silence, the darkness of the night seemed to close in around them. Mona's heart ached with the knowledge that the man she loved was slipping away, consumed by the very life they had built together. The sense of doom was palpable, and she feared for their future.

"We need to find a way out, Omar," she whispered, her voice filled with desperation. "Before it's too late."

He nodded, his eyes filled with a mix of determination and despair. "We will, Mona. We have to."

But even as he said the words, the reality of their situation loomed large. The final betrayal had shattered their trust, and the road ahead was uncertain. Omar and Mona faced an uncertain future, their love tested by the harsh realities of their world.

The streets of Norfolk were unforgiving, but they held onto each other, their bond the only light in the darkness. Together, they would navigate the treacherous path ahead, fighting to find a way out of the chaos and build a future free from the violence and betrayal that had defined their lives.

Chapter 15: Downfall

The once-mighty empire that Omar had built from the ground up was starting to crumble under the relentless pressure of law enforcement and the Junior Mafia. The twin assaults from both sides left him reeling, scrambling to keep control as everything he had worked for began to fall apart.

The police had not let up their crackdown. The arrests had continued, each one chipping away at Omar's network, each one leaving him more isolated and vulnerable. The Junior Mafia, emboldened by Omar's weakening position, intensified their efforts to take over his territory. They struck at his businesses, his suppliers, and his street-level operations with a ruthless efficiency that left Omar's crew struggling to keep up.

The financial strain was immense. Mona, who had once reveled in the luxury and power that came with Omar's empire, found herself desperately trying to hold onto their remaining assets. She spent her days on the phone with lawyers, accountants, and anyone who could help them navigate the legal and financial minefield they were in.

"Omar, we can't keep hemorrhaging money like this," she said one evening, her voice thick with stress and exhaustion. "We're running out of options. If we don't find a way to stabilize things, we're going to lose everything."

Omar, slumped in a chair with his head in his hands, looked up at her with tired eyes. "I know, Mona. I know. But every time I think I've got a handle on things, something else comes up. The Junior Mafia's not letting up, and the cops are on us 24/7. I don't know how much more I can take."

Mona knelt beside him, taking his hands in hers. "We have to stay strong, Omar. We can't give up now. We've come too far."

But even as she said the words, she could feel the weight of their situation pressing down on her. The stress was taking a toll on her, both emotionally and physically. She was losing weight, barely sleeping, and constantly on edge. The life they had built together was crumbling, and she felt powerless to stop it.

Omar was faring no better. The constant pressure had turned him into a shell of the man he once was. The confident, powerful leader who had commanded respect and fear was now consumed by paranoia and exhaustion. He had become short-tempered and irritable, lashing out at those around him, including Mona.

One night, after another exhausting day of trying to salvage what was left of their empire, Omar snapped. "Why are you always on my back, Mona? I'm doing everything I can to fix this, but it's never enough for you!"

Mona, already on the brink, couldn't hold back her own anger. "I'm on your back because we're losing everything, Omar! And you just keep making the same mistakes! We can't keep going like this!"

Their argument escalated, the stress and frustration boiling over. Harsh words were exchanged, words that cut deep and left lasting scars. When it was over, they both felt even more defeated than before, the weight of their crumbling empire driving a wedge between them.

As the days turned into weeks, the situation grew more dire. The Junior Mafia's attacks became more brazen, and the police were closing in on Omar with every passing day. Mona's attempts to hold onto their assets became increasingly futile, and she watched helplessly as everything they had built slipped through their fingers.

One afternoon, as she was going over their finances, Mona received a call from their lawyer. The news was devastating. "Mona, I'm sorry, but there's nothing more we can do. The government is seizing your assets. The bank accounts, the properties, everything."

Mona felt the world tilt around her. "What about the house? Our home?"

The lawyer's voice was sympathetic but firm. "I'm afraid that too. There's nothing left to protect."

She hung up the phone, numb with shock. She looked around the house, their sanctuary, and realized it was all over. The empire Omar had built, the life they had lived, was gone.

That evening, she broke the news to Omar. He took it with a grim acceptance, as if he had already known this was coming. "I guess this is it, then," he said quietly, staring at the floor.

Mona sat beside him, her own despair mirrored in his eyes. "What do we do now, Omar? Where do we go from here?"

He sighed, a sound filled with resignation and sorrow. "I don't know, Mona. I really don't know."

The physical and emotional toll on both of them was immense. The stress had aged them, turned them into shadows of their former selves. They had fought so hard to hold onto their empire, but in the end, it had been ripped away from them piece by piece.

As they sat together in the silence of their once-grand home, the realization of their downfall settled over them like a heavy blanket. The dream they had chased, the life they had built, was gone. All that was left was the stark reality of their situation and the uncertainty of what came next.

But even in the face of their downfall, they held onto each other. Their love, though battered and bruised, was the one thing that had endured. And in the darkness of their new reality, it was the only light they had left.

Chapter 16: A Desperate Escape

The weight of their crumbling empire pressed down on Mona like a suffocating blanket. The life she had shared with Omar, once filled with luxury and power, had become a nightmare of violence and betrayal. She knew they couldn't continue like this. The stress, the fear, and the constant threat of death were taking their toll. It was time for a desperate escape.

Late one night, as the city of Norfolk slept, Mona laid out her plan to Omar. They sat at the kitchen table, the room dimly lit by a single, flickering bulb. Omar's face was gaunt, shadows accentuating the lines of worry and exhaustion etched into his features.

"Omar, we need to get out. We can't keep living like this," Mona said, her voice steady but urgent. "We have to leave Norfolk, disappear, and start fresh somewhere else."

Omar looked at her, his eyes hollow. "Mona, I don't know if we can. The Junior Mafia, the cops—they'll never stop looking for us."

Mona reached across the table, taking his hand in hers. "We have to try. If we stay, we're dead. We need to leave now, before it's too late."

Omar took a deep breath, the weight of the decision pressing down on him. "Alright. We'll do it. But we need a plan."

Over the next few days, they worked in secret, gathering what little money they had left, securing fake IDs, and planning their route out of the city. They would leave under the cover of night, taking only what they could carry. It was a risk, but it was their only chance at survival.

As the day of their escape approached, the tension grew palpable. Every sound, every shadow seemed like a threat. Mona could barely sleep, her mind racing with fear and anticipation. Omar remained focused, his determination to protect Mona and give them a chance at a new life driving him forward.

The night of their escape was dark and stormy, the rain falling in heavy sheets that obscured the city. It was the perfect cover. Mona and

Omar slipped out of their home, their bags packed with essentials, and made their way to a waiting car. The plan was to drive to a safe house on the outskirts of the city, then switch vehicles and head for a new life far from Norfolk.

But the Junior Mafia was always one step ahead. As they approached the safe house, headlights suddenly blazed through the rain, blocking their path. Omar slammed on the brakes, and the car skidded to a halt.

"Get down!" Omar shouted, pulling Mona to the floor as bullets tore through the air.

The sound of gunfire was deafening, the car's windows shattering around them. Omar grabbed his gun, returning fire as he shielded Mona with his body. "We need to get out of here!" he yelled over the noise.

Mona nodded, her heart pounding in her chest. They crawled out of the car, using the cover of darkness and rain to their advantage. Omar fired at the attackers, creating a distraction long enough for Mona to make a run for the nearby alley.

"Go, Mona! I'll cover you!" Omar shouted.

Mona ran, her breath coming in ragged gasps. She reached the alley, turning to see Omar following close behind, still firing at the Junior Mafia. Just as he reached her, a bullet grazed his shoulder, and he stumbled, but he kept moving.

"Are you okay?" Mona cried, her eyes wide with fear.

"I'm fine," Omar grunted, clutching his shoulder. "Keep moving!"

They navigated the maze of alleys and backstreets, their pursuers close behind. The rain made the ground slick, and the darkness was disorienting, but they pressed on, driven by the desperate need to survive.

Finally, they reached an abandoned warehouse. Omar forced the door open, and they slipped inside, the silence and darkness a stark contrast to the chaos outside. They took a moment to catch their breath, their bodies trembling with adrenaline and fear.

"We can't stay here long," Omar whispered, his voice hoarse. "They'll find us."

Mona nodded, her mind racing. "We need to keep moving, find another way out of the city."

As they prepared to leave the warehouse, the sound of footsteps echoed through the empty space. Omar raised his gun, his eyes scanning the darkness. "They're here," he whispered.

The final showdown was inevitable. The Junior Mafia had tracked them, and there was no escaping the confrontation. Omar and Mona moved through the warehouse, their senses heightened, every sound a potential threat.

The attackers came in waves, their silhouettes barely visible in the dim light. Omar fired, his aim steady despite his injury. Mona stayed close, her own gun ready. The warehouse echoed with the sounds of gunfire and shouts, the violence a brutal reminder of the life they were trying to leave behind.

Omar took down one attacker after another, his determination fueled by the need to protect Mona. But the Junior Mafia was relentless, and the fight seemed endless. Just when it seemed they might be overwhelmed, a moment of clarity struck Mona.

"There! The back door!" she shouted, pointing to a barely visible exit.

Omar nodded, covering her as they made their way to the door. They burst through it, the cold night air hitting them like a wall. They ran, the sounds of pursuit growing fainter behind them. Finally, they reached a hidden car Omar had stashed as a backup plan. They jumped in, and Omar started the engine, peeling away from the warehouse.

As they sped away, the realization of their narrow escape washed over them. They were battered, bruised, but alive. The road ahead was uncertain, filled with unknown dangers and challenges, but they were ready to face it together.

Mona looked at Omar, her eyes filled with determination and love. "We did it. We're free."

Omar glanced at her, a small smile breaking through his exhaustion. "Yeah, we did. Now let's get the hell out of here."

They drove into the night, leaving behind the violence and chaos that had defined their lives. It was a desperate escape, but it was their chance at a new beginning. And for the first time in a long time, hope flickered in their hearts.

Chapter 17: Closure and Consequences

The aftermath of the final confrontation left a grim reality for Omar and Mona. The violent clash with the Junior Mafia had been brutal, with significant losses on both sides. The once-mighty empire that Omar had built lay in ruins, and the streets of Norfolk were forever scarred by the bloodshed.

As the dawn broke, casting a pale light over the city, the full extent of the battle became clear. Bodies lay strewn across the ground, the air heavy with the smell of gunpowder and death. Omar and Mona, exhausted and battered, had managed to escape the immediate danger, but the consequences of their actions were far from over.

It wasn't long before the police, drawn by the sound of gunfire and reports from terrified residents, descended upon the scene. Omar knew they had little time. They had to keep moving, find a way to disappear. But fate had other plans.

They were intercepted by a squad of police cars blocking the road. With no other choice, Omar stopped the car, his hands gripping the steering wheel tightly. He looked at Mona, his eyes filled with sorrow and regret. "Mona, I'm sorry."

Tears welled up in her eyes as she reached out to touch his face. "We did what we had to do, Omar. We tried."

As the police approached, guns drawn, Omar stepped out of the car, his hands raised in surrender. "Don't shoot! We're unarmed!"

The officers quickly took Omar into custody, slamming him against the hood of the car as they cuffed him. Mona was pulled from the passenger seat, her own hands cuffed behind her back. The weight of their downfall pressed heavily upon them as they were driven away, the city they had fought so hard to control now their captor.

The legal battle that followed was long and grueling. Omar faced a litany of charges, from drug trafficking to conspiracy to murder. The evidence against him was overwhelming, and despite the efforts of his high-priced lawyer, the outcome was all but certain. The courtroom was filled with a palpable tension, the weight of Omar's crimes laid bare for all to see.

Mona, though not directly involved in the operations, was also charged with aiding and abetting. The prosecution painted a damning picture of her involvement, portraying her as a willing participant in Omar's criminal empire. She sat in the courtroom, listening to the testimonies and the evidence, her heart heavy with the reality of her choices.

During the long months of the trial, Mona had plenty of time to reflect on her past. She thought about the allure of the streets, the seductive promise of power and wealth that had drawn her in. She remembered the early days with Omar, when everything had seemed possible, and the world had been theirs for the taking.

But as the trial progressed, she couldn't ignore the darker side of their life. The violence, the betrayal, the constant fear—it had all taken its toll. She had seen friends and allies gunned down, watched as their empire crumbled under the weight of its own corruption. And now, she faced the consequences of those choices.

Mona's introspection led her to a painful realization: the streets had shaped her, but they didn't define her. She had been caught in a cycle of violence and greed, but she had the power to break free. She thought about the future, about what kind of life she wanted to build once the trial was over.

One day, during a break in the proceedings, Mona sat in her cell, staring at the ceiling. She thought about the people she had lost, the friends who had died, and the life she had left behind. Tears rolled down her cheeks as she whispered to herself, "I have to be better. I have to do better."

The trial eventually concluded, and the verdict was delivered. Omar was found guilty on all counts and sentenced to life in prison without the possibility of parole. Mona received a lesser sentence, but she still faced years behind bars. As she was led away from the courtroom, she glanced back at Omar, their eyes meeting one last time.

"We'll get through this," Omar mouthed, his eyes filled with determination and regret.

Mona nodded, her heart breaking. "I love you," she whispered, before the door closed between them.

In the years that followed, Mona worked hard to rebuild her life. She participated in rehabilitation programs, sought therapy, and found solace in helping others who had been caught in similar cycles of violence and crime. She used her time in prison to reflect on her past and plan for a future free from the shadows of her former life.

The journey was long and difficult, but Mona was determined to make it. She knew that the choices she had made had led her to this point, but she also believed in the possibility of redemption and change. She held onto the hope that, one day, she could leave the past behind and build a new life, one defined not by the streets, but by her strength and resilience.

The aftermath of the final confrontation had been devastating, but it also offered a chance for closure and a new beginning. As Mona looked forward to the future, she carried with her the lessons of her past, the scars of her experiences, and the determination to rise above them.

Chapter 18: New Beginnings and Final Reflections

Mona had served her time, and the day she walked out of prison, she felt the weight of the world lift off her shoulders. The sky seemed bluer, the air fresher, and the sense of freedom was overwhelming. She had spent countless nights dreaming of this moment, and now it was finally here. But with freedom came the daunting task of starting over, of building a new life from the ashes of her old one.

The streets of Norfolk were both familiar and foreign to her. The city had changed in her absence. New faces had taken over old territories, and the names of Omar and Mona were whispered less frequently. Some people still remembered their reign, the power and fear they commanded, but others had moved on, swept away by the ever-changing tides of the street life.

Mona found solace in the small things. She rented a modest apartment and found a job at a local community center, helping at-risk youth avoid the pitfalls that had ensnared her. It was a far cry from the life of luxury she had once known, but it was honest work, and it gave her a sense of purpose.

One afternoon, as she walked through the neighborhood, she passed by the spots where she and Omar had once held court. The memories flooded back: the highs of their power, the lows of their betrayals, the constant threat of violence that had hung over their heads. She thought about the price they had paid for their empire, and the toll it had taken on their love.

The community had moved on, but the scars of their past were still visible. Some people nodded in recognition when they saw her, while others looked away, their expressions a mix of pity and disdain. Mona understood. She had been both a queen and a pariah, revered and reviled in equal measure.

As she walked, she reflected on the journey that had brought her here. The highs had been intoxicating: the money, the power, the sense of invincibility. But the lows had been devastating: the betrayals, the violence, the constant fear. She had lost friends, allies, and the man she loved. The price of power had been steep, and she had paid it in full.

One evening, she sat by the window of her apartment, looking out at the city lights. The same lights that had once symbolized their empire now seemed distant, almost mocking. She thought about Omar, still locked away, paying the price for their choices. She missed him every day, but she knew that their love had been built on a foundation of sand. The streets had shaped them, but they didn't define them.

Mona's journey toward a new life was filled with challenges, but it was also filled with hope. She had learned from her past, and she was determined to build a better future. She focused on her work, helping young people find a way out of the cycle of violence and crime. She shared her story, not as a cautionary tale, but as a testament to resilience and the possibility of redemption.

The community slowly moved on, new stories and new players taking the stage. The legend of Omar and Mona became just another chapter in the ever-evolving saga of the streets. Some people remembered them as cautionary tales, while others saw them as symbols of the dangers of unchecked ambition. Mona was content to let the past stay in the past, focusing instead on the future she was building.

In her final reflections, Mona understood that the price of power had been too high. The love she and Omar had shared had been real, but it had been tainted by the world they lived in. Survival in the streets had demanded sacrifices that left them both scarred. But in the end, she had emerged stronger, more resilient, and determined to make a difference.

The journey had been long and painful, but it had also been enlightening. Mona had faced her demons, and she had come out the other side with a new sense of purpose. She knew that the road ahead would not be easy, but she was ready to face it head-on, armed with the lessons of her past and the strength of her convictions.

As she sat by the window, the city lights twinkling in the distance, Mona felt a sense of peace. She had survived the streets, the betrayals, and the heartbreak. She had found a way to move forward, to build a new life on her terms. And in the end, that was all that mattered.

The story of Omar and Mona was one of love and loss, power and betrayal. But it was also a story of resilience and hope. Mona had found her way out of the darkness, and she was determined to help others do the same. The streets had taken much from her, but they had also given her the strength to rise above. And as she looked out at the city that had once been her kingdom, she knew that she was finally free.

Don't miss out!

Visit the website below and you can sign up to receive emails whenever Rachael Reed publishes a new book. There's no charge and no obligation.

https://books2read.com/r/B-A-WXARB-BPKPD

BOOKS2READ

Connecting independent readers to independent writers.

Also by Rachael Reed

Codefendant
Codefendant
Once a Cheater
Once a Cheater
Passport Bro
What Happens in Prison
Preference
Sprinkle Sprinkle
Championship Bad
Street Exodus
Street Exodus
Street Royalty
Pawns of Power